Brilliant Bob is Curious

Written by
Kenneth T Jolivet

Copyright © 2021 by Kenneth T Jolivet

ISBN: 978-1-7365139-3-4

Edited by Melissa Peitsch

Illustrated by Renata Christine

Book Layout by Solaja Slobodan

Brilliant Bob just woke up
from a great night's sleep.

It was Saturday: Bob's day
to play with friends.

Brilliant Bob ate his tasty breakfast,
said goodbye to his mom and dad,
and headed out to play.

"Oh, but don't forget about Leo,"
said his mom to Bob.

Leo, the families' Black Labrador
puppy dog, was wagging his tail
and jumping with joy, trying to get
Brilliant Bob's attention.

It worked!

A few minutes later, Brilliant Bob
was at Genuine George's house.

He knocked on the door.

Genuine George opened it and smiled.

"Hey George, let's go exploring
outside.
I'm feeling lucky."

"Great idea Bob," said Genuine
George. "But first, I need to
check with my mom and dad."

George's parents gave their permission, with the advice to be careful, stick together, and not talk to strangers.

Off they went: fresh and full of energy.

It was a beautiful day.

They walked along the neighborhood streets they knew so well.

They were headed to the small forest nearby.

"Wait, what's this?" Bob asked. "Is someone throwing away a bike?"

Brilliant Bob saw a dirty bike leaning up against a trashcan that stood on the sidewalk in front of a house.

Bob was curious!

Why would someone throw away a bike?

Just to be sure it was okay to take the bike, Bob knocked on the door and asked the people if he could have it.

They said yes and were very happy that someone wanted it.

Brilliant Bob jumped on the bike and gave it a test ride.
It seemed to work just fine.

Bob was very excited.

He knew that once he cleaned it up, it would be a good bike.

"Hey, let me have a go," said George.

He rode it around a bit and agreed...the bike was great!

They rode it to Dazzling Dave's and Superboy Sam's houses.

Bob wanted to show off his lucky find.

Naturally, Dave and Sam each wanted to try it out, and Brilliant Bob let them.

The four boys took turns riding that bike for hours.

They had so much fun!

It was a great day, but it was getting late and it was time to go home and eat dinner.

That night, as Bob lay down to sleep, he got to thinking.

What makes the bike move? How does it stop? How do the gears and chain work? How do the pedals rotate?

There was so much he wanted to know, and he decided he was going to take the bike apart and figure it out.

Brilliant Bob was very curious!

Since Genuine George was such a clever boy and good friend, Brilliant Bob decided to ask George to help him find the answers to his questions.

He was sure they could do it together.

Brilliant Bob woke up pumped and ready. He couldn't wait to tell Genuine George his plan.

Before leaving the house Bob asked his dad if he could use some of his tools.

"Of course Bob," his dad said. "I'll get you set up after we all clear up the breakfast dishes."

Genuine George had also just finished his family breakfast when the doorbell rang.

George opened the door.

"Hey Brilliant Bob, what's going on," asked George.

"Lots! I have a great idea.
Would you like to help me take my new bike apart and rebuild it?
I'm very curious how a bike works."

"Wow, what a great idea!" Genuine George said. "You know I love to discover and learn. I'm always curious."

"Excellent," said Bob. "I knew you were just the boy for the job. Let's go."

It took Brilliant Bob and Genuine George most of the day to take the bike apart.

They found that if they took their time and used the right tools, things came apart quite easily.

The trick was to carefully lay the pieces down on the ground in the same order they came out.

They also took notes and pictures as they went along, so they would know how it went back together.

Brilliant Bob had a master plan.

Not only did he want to know how the bike worked...He also wanted to make the bike better, using better parts.

He asked his dad to take them to the junkyard to look for good parts from other bikes that had been thrown away.

Brilliant Bob knew he could find bikes that had been thrown away for various reasons, but still with many other perfectly good parts.

And he was right.

Bob and George found new handlebars, a seat and seat post, pedals, forks, a crankset, brakes, wheels, and ball bearings for the hub.

It was time to rebuild the bike.

But it was getting late.

They'd have to wait until the next weekend to start rebuilding the bike.

In the meantime, all the other kids at school heard about what Brilliant Bob and Genuine George had done.

Most of the kids thought they were crazy for ruining such a good bike. The girls especially seemed to have less curiosity or desire to do such a thing.

"How could you two boys be so destructive and ungrateful to such a lucky find?" many said.

This lack of understanding didn't put Bob or George off their goal to rebuild the bike better than it was before.

They were going to show everyone what could be done with curiosity and the need to discover and learn.

All they had to do was research online and watch lots of videos, and they could learn all they needed.

Deep inside, Brilliant Bob felt he was doing the right thing.

It was in his blood.

It was in George's blood too.

And it was in Dave's and Sam's nature to also want to know how things worked.

Brilliant Bob, Dazzling Dave, Genuine George and Superboy Sam were four very curious boys.

Every evening, after they did their
homework and finished dinner,
Bob and George got together
to study bike mechanics and repairs.

They found there was so much
material on the Internet and they
loved the online demonstration videos.

They were amazed seeing other
people who were doing what they
were doing: being curious, and
finding out how bikes work
and rebuilding them.

After five nights of studying hard,
Brilliant Bob and Genuine
George felt ready to tackle
the bike's assembly.

Saturday morning soon arrived.

It was *show time!*

They started with the most difficult part first: the ball-bearing assembly and crankset.

If they could do this, the rest would be much easier.

They put the pieces together, using the reverse order from when they took it apart last Sunday.

For reassurance, they followed along with a video.

It worked!

They put the most difficult part together with all the pieces: and no leftovers.

Oh, but what a greasy mess...

Who cares? It was fun!

Next was the rear wheel hub. Done.
Then, the new front fork, stem and
handlebars.
Not too bad. Check.

Now, to replace the brake
system: It was rather tricky,
but with patience and much
trial and error, they got it done.

Pedals, seat post and seat.

Check.

Next, it was time to put the wheels
to the forks and axle. Done.

Finally, they put the chain
back on the bike.

Check.

The bike was finished,
and it looked awesome!

It was time for the test ride.

Brilliant Bob and Genuine George took their bike out to the street.

Most of the other neighborhood kids were outside playing football.

They all stopped and looked when they saw Bob and George with their cool, rebuilt bike.

Bob jumped on the bike, pedalled hard to gain speed and then slammed on the brakes into a power slide that looked and sounded *very* cool.

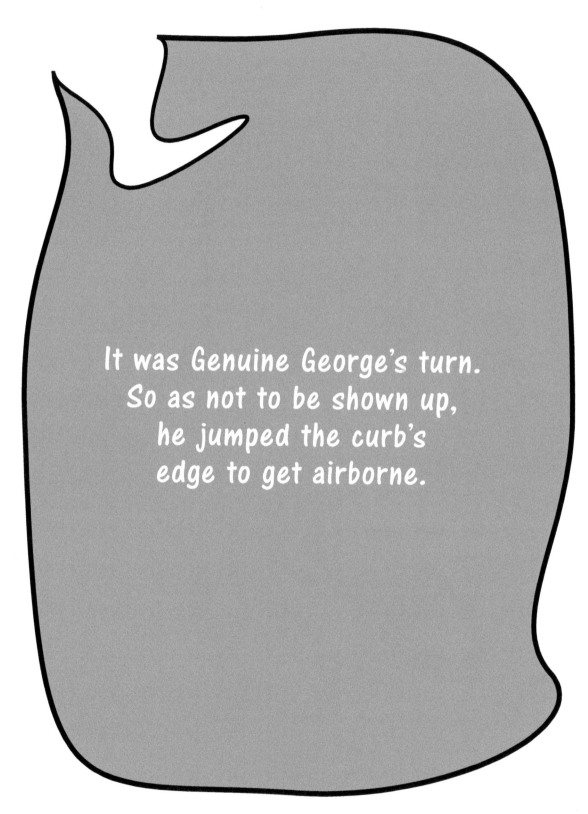

It was Genuine George's turn.
So as not to be shown up,
he jumped the curb's
edge to get airborne.

Everyone was amazed.

It was a great day and, in truth,
Bob and George enjoyed showing off.

Not because they were arrogant,
but because they were proud of
their achievements and new skills.

Brilliant Bob and Genuine George
learned several things since
the day they found that old,
dirty bike in the trash.

They both felt good about their inner
curiosity and the need to know
what makes things do what they do.

'High Five' to curiosity!

They discovered that curiosity
helps you learn things.

They discovered that destruction is a
part of curiosity and learning about
something.

They discovered that taking your
time on a project, instead of rushing,
helps you do things the right way.

They discovered that most projects
need a step-by-step process, and it's
okay to make mistakes along the way.

They discovered that mistakes
are great teachers...

Because you learn not to repeat them!

And on top of all that, they felt proud. After all, they had totally rebuilt a bike by themselves.

It wasn't easy, but they did their research and did not let fear of failure get to them.

Brilliant Bob and Genuine George felt the charge of confidence that only comes from doing something that takes time and hard work.

They had knowledge that no one could take from them: all because they were brave and curious.

That night in bed Brilliant Bob thought to himself:

If I can learn how to rebuild a bike, I can learn to rebuild a motorcycle.

If I can rebuild a motorcycle, I can learn to rebuild a car.

If I can rebuild a car, I can learn to rebuild a plane!

Brilliant Bob began to wonder how a jet engine worked.

"Man, curiosity is powerful and so cool."

Brilliant Bob thanks you for reading this book.

He also invites you to join him in his other great adventures where:

Brilliant Bob is Competitive
Brilliant Bob is Strong
Brilliant Bob is Brave
Brilliant Bob Takes a Risk
Brilliant Bob is Stoic
Brilliant Bob is Persistent

HIGH FIVE DUDE!

You can buy all seven books on Amazon.

And don't forget to visit Brilliant Bob's website at...

www.BrilliantBobKidBooks.com